Acknowledgments

I would like to thank Luciano Tempo and Carol and Danny Garcia, for keeping me alive throughout the years. To Rob Holt, my brother sculptor, and Sandy Yagyu, my sister swordsman, for listening, and to my dear wife, Catherine, for loving me through difficult times. Thanks also to my six children, my parents and siblings, and my extended family for their continuing support and faith. Special thanks to Tom Ayers, M'Lynn Geren, Miki Myamoto, Coach Grant, Sal Ferantelli, Donald Eugene Rowe, Robert "Scotty" Holt, Charles Fischer, Alex Prokepenko, James Campbell, Martha and Beth, Mary and Dianna, Barney and Lexanne, and the entire Sand City gang for their enduring inspiration. Finally, another special thanks to my dear mother, without whose help this book would never have seen the light of day.

Introduction

If you're like me, you'll skip this introduction and go straight to the stories. But ... also like me, you might come back, intrigued by what this must say, after reading such unusual stuff.

I discovered the short story when I was young, and I was particularly drawn to science fiction. As I first opened a collection, I would always page through it looking for the shortest tale. I have always been taken with authors who can develop something interesting, hook you, and finally give you a payoff in the last sentence, all in a few pages or less.

Indeed, we seem to live in a time when the consumer wants everything *now*. I have been told many times that short stories are hard to market, that maybe I should add more detail and stretch things out a bit. I respectfully disagree. These stories, to me, are like scrumptious appetizers on a menu—not each a drawn-out meal, but fully satisfying in their own right nonetheless, down to the last crumb. Only one of them is a true story, written exactly as it happened.

This collection is intended to be read like many others: in no particular order. The stories are printed in the order they were written, not according to which was my favorite. They are like children; each one is my favorite. But ah! I digress ... let me tell you a short story about myself, and how the stories that follow came to be.

*

As I proceed through life, I am more and more convinced that everyone born into this world has been blessed with at least one gift or talent. It's discovering just what this gift *is* that is the trick, I have found.

As a five-year-old, I felt my talent lay in the ability to fly (albeit for only a moment) after my mother had lovingly pinned a dish towel to my shirt for a cape and I had jumped off the back porch then ran with it streaming behind me. In Sunday school I struck gold the first time I opened my mouth to sing. Every song seemed to be my favorite, and it was here, I think, that the seed of wanting to be a performer in life was sown in me.

At fourteen, I landed a job at a place where my older brother had worked, Monterey Sculpture Studio, at the southern end of Cannery Row. It was an artist's cooperative and bronze foundry, a fascinating place for a young boy to be. I was the all-around gofer there, and I was also trained in the bronze casting process. Some ten years later, I was hired by one of the artists I had met there to work with him—for the next fifteen years, it turned out—as his apprentice.

During this time I can remember thinking to myself that I would work at this job only until I could find what my true talent in life was. But after my boss and mentor, Scotty, died and I took over his small concern, I figured that I should call myself a metal sculptor and be done with it. It seems at times that life, though, is not done with us, even though we think otherwise.

I found myself, at forty-five, sitting on the local city council (a position I had held for nearly twenty years), still hammering out my creations in a small studio. But then one day my world was turned upside down. I had been thrown more than a few curveballs in life, but this was a particularly tough one: my daughter had run away from home. Suffice it to say, my family found her two months later hiding right under our noses, but those two months were agony for me. Something happened during her absence that I cannot now explain. I had started to write these stories.

It's strange, the things that inspire our creative minds. There are endless things in life that will spark the creative process in us, but tragedy seems to be a most powerful one. Like a phoenix rising from the ashes, during that dark time I found life and hope in putting pen to paper to produce the stories you hold here, and I continue to write today. I'm not sure just where many of these stories came from, although I get asked that all the time. I have, though, found the most sublime joy in discovering each one—from that first tiny seed of an idea, to what you see here.

You and I are *all* writers, my friends, writing our lives one moment at a time. May your story have the most fulfilling surprise of all.

Enjoy!
Craig Hubler

"Purr-haps"

It was Cate's longest standing relationship, she always told me, and being her husband, I am not afraid to say I was somewhat jealous. We had been married for four years, and Ozzie, her black male tom, had been with her ten.

She was a talker—no doubt about it. Often I was so fascinated by her long, auburn hair and the way her tiny hands danced about in the air that she would catch me nodding and mumbling a dumb "uh-huh," just to appease her, when actually nothing had penetrated into that part of my brain that does the comprehending. She said cats were good for conversation, and I would just smile and nod. "Just as long as it makes her happy," was my motto.

One day, I realized I had left a receipt on my desk, so I swung back by to pick it up. It was 3:00 PM, an odd time for me to be home. As I walked through the house, I heard Cate talking to someone and followed the sound of her sweet voice to the laundry room. My footsteps, muffled by the plush carpet, gave no warning as I came to the door. Just as I was peeking around the corner, I heard a single word spoken by a strange, high, raspy voice coming from above the washing machine on a high shelf. "Perhaps …" the voice said, just before I saw the speaker—Ozzie.

As I stared at him in disbelief, a silent but unmistakable message was conveyed: "You may think you heard something, but you'll *never* know." Cate raised her eyebrows and looked at the floor, a smug smirk planted firmly on her face.

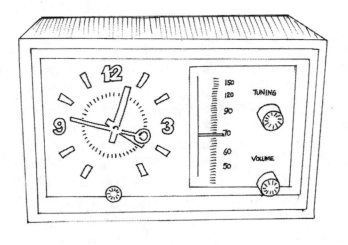

The Inheritance

Maria had worked for the brute for most of a year now. After having worked in the fields and washed dishes at a local dive, it was the best thing she could find to support herself and her five-year-old daughter, Esperanza. Being a maid for a rich, angry man, she thought, was not so bad a thing to be most days.

On this particular day, just as she finished dressing her daughter in their meager room, Maria heard the front door slam—a noise that shook the entire house. "Boss man angry today, Essy," she whispered to her daughter, kneeling.

He had, in fact, just returned from meeting with an attorney, who had read him "The Will." He had waited years now for his father's demise, to discover just what permanent riches awaited him. Maria had endured his cruel streak for many months. Endured it with a quiet patience that would have amazed even Mother Teresa.

Now he was on a rampage, stomping through his small kingdom, screaming obscenities Maria had never heard. "A lousy clock!" he shouted, stamping his foot like a child. "The man was a millionaire five hundred times over, and I get a lousy clock!"

He flung the small clock radio in Maria's direction. She raised her hands with a cry, "Iy, iy, iy!" and was lucky enough to catch it before it hit the floor.

"Take the damned thing away!" he shouted as he stormed out of the room. Maria turned to go, and quietly walking from the room, she heard him shout at her from down the hall, "Don't you forget, Maria, tomorrow is my birthday, and I want you up early to prepare for the party!"

That night Maria took the misbegotten clock and plugged it in. With a happy hum and a few turns of the dial, she set the clock to wake her on the morn.

The clock ... did not wake her. It seemed the thing did not even work for keeping time, and as a result, Maria was fired and on the street. A hundred dollars severance pay and all of their belongings in one bag, she and her daughter checked into a cheap hotel. There Maria sat on the bed to take toll of all they had. Not much. Finally Maria came across the clock. "Well ... at least I can try and fix this," she said to Esperanza, who sat quietly by the window playing with her only doll.

Maria removed a small knife from her purse and opened from its fold a screwdriver, with which she began to remove the back of the clock. As the plastic cover hit the floor, Esperanza heard a gasping sound so unfamiliar that it startled her. Dropping her doll, she ran to her mother's side and peered into the clock.

"Essy," Maria quivered, "look! Look and see what I have found!"

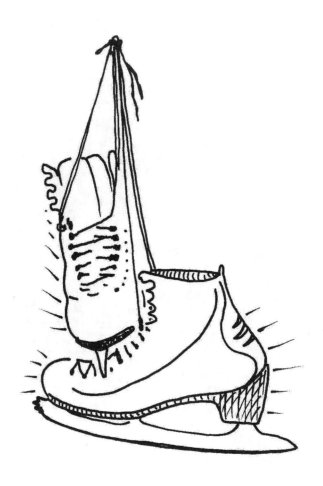

The Golden Prize

No one on the Olympic ice skating committee had ever come across the name of Mai Soo Kim, but what they had before them was impressive enough. Going over the list of ladies singles contestants who had qualified to compete, the committee had seen Mai Soo Kim's name and drawn a complete blank.

"Really now," implored the chairman, "at this level of competition, surely at least one of you has seen this young woman skate?" There was a brief uncomfortable silence as those present looked at one another with nothing but blank stares.

"Well, sir," the secretary finally said, "the only thing we have besides her application is a video of a previous performance."

After another ten minutes, during which the footage was played, all agreed she was a most accomplished skater—certainly more than adequate for competition. A few more queries and checks, and she was entered, and then she was for the most part forgotten.

*

Months passed, and the much-awaited Olympics opened with the usual fanfare. Some days later, and to the surprise of many, Mai Soo found herself placed in the top ten skating contestants. Suddenly the world was abuzz. All of the networks began to dig up anything they could find on her, yet all came away with maddeningly little. Interviews with her were polite, yes, but she seemed distant and gave out little of use to any reporter. The video clips that the committee held were distributed throughout the media, who made bleak attempts to put together any kind of segment to show the world just who this young woman was. There was not much to show, but then again, few expected her to medal.

And no one in the world expected what she had in store for her final program.

As Mai Soo took to the ice for her final skate, commentators again speculated and played up what little they knew. As with all skaters, she had submitted an outline of the various moves she would be attempting. Music drifted across the ice, and the lithe young woman began her long program.

"A good, clean skate," was how most reported it as she conducted her performance. Nothing spectacular, but technically flawless. Then, just before the end, Mai Soo Kim did something that stunned everyone.

It is generally known in the world of professional ice skating that a triple axle performed correctly takes an average of 1.2 seconds. Mai Soo Kim's … took three. The difference was so bewildering to the judges and the audience that an audible, unanimous sigh was let out in the arena, broadcast to all the world. Its effect was *stunning*, and it secured for Mai Soo Kim, despite all of the previous and following performances by other skaters, the gold medal.

The crowd cheered the new champion as the reward was placed around her neck while the appropriate anthem was played, yet instead of smiles or tears, most who watched that day would remember only a faraway look in the skater's eyes. Reporters scrambled feverishly to interview her after, yet she was nowhere to be found. Mai Soo had slipped away ...

*

Far above the earth, hidden from view, a most unusual ship took on a beautiful young woman. Walking briskly to the bridge, she met its captain, saluted, and removed the shiny gold medal from around her neck. "Mission accomplished, sir," she said as she handed the prize to her superior.

"Finally," spoke captain Vartoo. "I've always wanted to see one of these. Well done, Mai Soo, well done!"

Friends

Paulo had finally found his oasis. Having made a tidy fortune in small appliances, the fifty-something bachelor looked ever forward to his next visit to the paradise he had discovered just weeks after retiring.

A small spa in a sometime balmy California coastal town had caught his eye one day, and after the first visit, Paulo knew he had found the most sublime way to unwind. It was equipped with two large tubs and an enormous sauna, in which he delighted in sweating out whatever ailed him and even belting out a Broadway tune, whenever he found himself alone.

The best part of the place, however, was the gardens. He marveled at the myriad plants and flowers that were so mindfully tended to there. His favorite by far was a large banana palm. Its fronds were wide and many, providing him with the most wonderful shade. Throughout the day, from the time he arrived till he left, its canopy would play shadows in a gentle arc across the lawn, and he would gladly rearrange his towel to follow its protection.

During his visits, Paulo would always take the time to practice his yoga routine, stretching and posing in a most extraordinary way. It did not take long for the majestic palm to *notice* this—and to respond with a show of its own.

One spring day, Paulo saw something remarkable about his palm: a flower was growing out of its center.

"What have we here?" he mused out loud as he stood gazing, hands on hips, with a towel wrapped around his firm waist and an old straw hat perched on his thinning hair.

The flower was unusually large, about the size of a human head, its petals a dark maroon that was nearly black. Perhaps the most amazing thing of all, to Paulo, was to sit quietly and watch it bloom. In just ten minutes its inner petals would open to reveal yet another bud within. He could tell by counting the old petals that led into the flower's center that it had bloomed like so twenty-seven times.

Soon, other guests of the spa and the management were also intrigued, and they began to watch in eager anticipation for the next layer of the flower to reveal itself. Some thought at first that it flowered daily, but then it would miss a day, then sometimes two, then it would flower three days in a row. No one realized that the palm only put on its elegant display when Paulo was there to watch. Again and again it bloomed, and it began to look very much like something out of a Dr. Seuss book. Then one day, it stopped blooming altogether, and Paulo never returned. Lured by tropical climes, he had moved away. Soon after, the old banana palm died, and it was hewn down and chopped up for compost. Its sudden absence was noticed and mourned by many.

*

Not far from a sandy shore on a humid island in paradise, Paulo reached for his old straw hat and removed from it a napkin that he then carefully unwrapped to reveal a small seed. This he carefully planted in the fertile soil outside his newly acquired cabana.

"How strange," he thought, "that by chance this seed should fall into my hat on the lawn of the spa the last day I was there."

Only the *palm* knew that it did nothing by chance.

The Sleep Talkers

It was Julie's first place of her own. Having finally graduated, and being comfortably employed, she had found an apartment. She enjoyed the solitude of her new-old place; it was old because her apartment was actually part of a stately, antique mansion that had been divided into three unusual pieces.

Her landlords were a friendly, senior couple who were also her next-door neighbors. She had discovered almost immediately just how thin the walls were in the old abode. When she was still and there were no other distractions, she could hear the couple's voices as if they were standing on the other side of the room. Mildly annoying at first, Julie dismissed this inconvenience after the first day or so, learning, for the most part, to ignore it. Her neighbors were so low-key that the only time she really noticed anything bothersome was late at night, when they would both begin to snore.

Even that, though, was bearable, and Julie began to imagine that there were two monks next door chanting. Their routine soon became even a comfort to her, and she had no problems falling asleep to the gentle rise and fall of their snoring.

One night two weeks after she had moved in, just as she was falling asleep to the nocturnal duet, Julie was surprised to suddenly hear a voice. It was a man's voice, and then a woman's answered. At first she thought the pair had awoken for some reason and were talking about something, but she could hear also, in between their words, their gentle snores. She knew then, bizarre as it seemed, that they were talking to one another in their sleep! Not only that, but the dialogue continued all … night … long.

On the morn, as Julie was preparing to go to work on what little sleep she had gotten, her friend Jill came by to say hi and to make plans for later on. "You look terrible, Julie," she said.

"Didn't sleep much," Julie replied in between sips of coffee. "The two next door kept me up most of the night, talking. I could have asked them to quiet down, but," she smirked and shook her head, "they were both asleep!"

*

When Bob and Bonnie had met, though only thirty-seven at the time, Bob had already been through a seventeen-year marriage—and had five children, to boot. Bonnie was ten years his senior and had never been married or had children of her own. As the relationship had bloomed, all of the reasons they thought a union for them wouldn't work melted away. Now twenty years later, they were celebrating their anniversary in a most romantic way.

They kept mostly to themselves these days, living in the old estate that Bonnie had inherited a few years back. With some help, Bob had been able to split the house into three spaces, and just two weeks prior they had rented the last space, the one next to them, to a nice young woman.

After a full day consisting of a picnic, a walk, dinner, and dancing, they lay in bed reminiscing before falling asleep. "I know I've said this before, Bonnie, but I would love to have known you when you were a teenager."

"I was too wild back then," she answered. "But *you*, I think, would have definitely been worth knowing."

As they drifted off into dreamland, a higher power intervened and gave them, that night, an extraordinary gift. They both had the exact same dream, at the exact same time.

Morning found them wrapped in each other's arms, and when they awoke and stared into one another's eyes, they smiled together, knowing not a word need be spoken.

*

"So!" said Jill, absolutely fascinated now, "what did they say, what did they say?"

"That's the crazy part," said Julie. "They sounded … like a couple of teenagers!"

The Poppies Are Blooming

Minnie drove west through the stifling heat of a small southern California town. Music filled her car and spilled out through open windows as she sped along winding roads. "The heart is abloom … it shoots up through the stony ground …"

She was escaping work this day, and trying desperately to escape something else that had been rotting inside of her for years. Word had got out that since the spring rains had fallen, the poppies were beginning to bloom.

As she came around one particular bend, Minnie finally saw what she had driven miles for: a gentle sea of orange wonder. This was the best spot any poppy admirer had found to stand and gaze for a while at nature's magnificent show. It only lasted for a short time, but while it did, so many from all over came to see it. Minnie pulled over and strode casually toward the gently undulating crowd …

*

He was a solitary man who relished his privacy. Working most of his life as an engineer had caused him to look at most things in a practical way. There was not much practical he could find this day, though, as he stood in a field of strangers. Every year for four years now he had left his metropolis and driven to a spot that, after a good rain, gave up a beauty that never failed to move something inside of him for the better. His wife had, after a brief illness, suddenly passed on, and only after wandering in grief for days had he found, with many others, the healing, orange tide.

As he stood gazing, he could not help but notice the young woman whose hair seemed to rival the blooming flowers. She saw his glance and admired for a moment his chiseled features and graying temples before taking a step toward him.

"They're just everywhere, aren't they?" she half-spoke in his direction.

"Yes, but the view is even better from just over there." He pointed.

"Minnie," she said. She reached out her hand, and that's how it began.

Right then and there, the forming of a bond was begun, and the two of them would share there among the poppies those things that lovers only dream of. After several hours and many stories, an unusual pact was made between the two, and then they went their separate ways.

*

Every year from then on, after the first spring rains, Minnie would start to check her mail for a small, cream-colored envelope with a message from a mysterious man. "The poppies are blooming," was all it would say, but it needed say nothing else. She knew what to do, then: drop everything and drive.

Year after year, they met at the same spot to share what each had to offer. He, the methodical engineer; she, a redheaded muse; both giving, both receiving a mutual healing that would fortify and sustain them until they met again.

Minnie was content in her respect for his privacy and did not seek him out beyond those hills. His faithful note was all she needed to keep her afloat and truly alive.

One day, several years after that first meeting, spring was coming. Minnie could feel it in the air. She read through the metro news that morning as she always did, coffee cup in hand, and hummed away to no particular tune. Then with a simple turn of a page, she came across a picture and an announcement. At that moment, time stopped, for her. She had found him at last where she least expected to: in the obituaries. At first she refused to believe it. She could not breathe, sliding from her living room chair to lie in a heap and weep for most of an hour.

Two weeks later, the rains came, and she did not care. She walked through the day in a daze, hardly looking up from the ground. As she went through her mail that day, she nearly tossed it aside—the now-familiar, cream-colored envelope. Tearing it open in disbelief, she read its simple note. "The poppies are blooming," it said, but then underneath was a new message: "Do not despair." Minnie ran for the car.

*

He knew he was dying. In his last weeks before leaving this world, motorists along the winding country road would notice a solitary man standing in the fields. Before him stood a surveyor's compass, and from time to time, he would peer into it, scribble down notes, pack it all up, and wander into the hills, only then to return later and peer some more. No one stopped to question, and no one really cared.

*

As Minnie came around the familiar bend that day, she saw a most unfamiliar sight. There had always been many who stopped at this prime viewing vista, but it seemed that day as if all of humanity had arrived.

She could feel something powerful begin to rise within her as she abandoned her car and strode briskly toward the crowd, which seemed to be gathered in a mass upon one particular spot—*their* spot. They were all pointing in the same direction, and sounds of amazement filled the air. As she arrived in their midst, she turned and saw it for herself. There, on the very hill they had gazed at for hours over the years, were thousands of red poppies in the perfect shape of a heart.

Rogé's Revenge

He had been working on his latest painting for weeks. This was somewhat unusual for Rogé, the slender Frenchman who was known to start and finish most of his works in just one day. He had risen quickly in the art world, a young graduate on fire, setting ablaze both critics and fans alike. So quickly had fame and fortune found him that many believed he had peaked and was on his way out, like last week's fresh flowers. That winter, one person in particular had come down quite hard on the artistic head of John P. Rogé. Marleigh Harris was an art critic for the major metropolitan daily that was published just a few hours' drive north of the young artist's hideaway.

Tucked away not far from a scenic California coastal highway was a modest cabin Rogé had purchased with money from his talents. He lived alone, and he relished the forest that surrounded his sanctuary. He had acquired enough property to wander in numerous directions for most of an hour without coming to the edge of what he owned. Nothing could please him more than sitting for long periods of time just watching the insects move from leaf to leaf, doing whatever it was that they did. An amateur entomologist from a young age, Rogé knew that at least he would never run out of subjects to study.

Marleigh's critique had bothered him, that day late in winter. Seeing his name coupled with terms like "artistic imbecile" and "immature renderings" made him feel as if someone a hundred miles away had reached out and slapped him in the face. He was incensed that someone could, with just a few words, make or break a career, in so many readers' eyes.

Not that he had never had a bad review. This, though, seemed to him an attack on something soft and precious inside of him, and it pulled a cold shade over his remote estate. That night he could not sleep, tossing in darkness, adjusting pillows and heaters through the night to no avail. Then, in the final hour before the sunrise, he slept, and dreamed, and finally woke to a revelation that caused him to whisper in joy.

That very day, he set out to paint his masterpiece and to right, in a very unusual way, a wrong.

Now, weeks later, he was nearly finished. He arranged, on a lovely spring day upcoming, to have ten of his closest friends over for a private showing. His guest list even included Mr. Harris, his artistic nemesis—the very man for whom he had secretly created his newest endeavor

All those invited arrived within an hour of each other that early spring afternoon, and each walked into Rogé's home eagerly expecting to see this new work right away. His cabin, after all, consisted of just one very large, elevated room, and there were not many places to hide his new piece. But nothing was mysteriously draped; just many of his colorful, familiar works adorned the place.

After a scrumptious meal and delicious conversation, the artist invited his guests to move to the living area, for them to sit among huge pillows, sip tea, and wonder. Where was the painting? Where indeed?

"You've been looking at it all day," quipped Rogé. Puzzled, polite outbursts escaped from all. "Right there," he said, pointing to the only blank wall in the place, ten feet high, fifteen feet wide.

"Pardon me, young man!" started the art critic. "I came here to …"

But Rogé cut him off with his slender hand, upraised and commanding a polite silence. He quietly strode to the huge windows that looked out into the lush forest, windows that hinged and swung in such a way as to allow one to view all that was beyond unencumbered.

"I began collecting paint some weeks ago," he began, "out there." He gestured to the lush forest beyond. "It was only this morning that I applied it to my canvas, because like you and I, ladies and gentlemen, *they* like it *fresh* …"

So began a show none there would ever forget. It began right away with a single butterfly fluttering through the grand, open windows and alighting on the blank wall. Within the hour there were hundreds of them clinging wherever Rogé had painted fresh nectar to the previously blank wall, creating such an amazing design that most, including the critic, could only sit and stare with mouths agape.

It was the most incredible thing Marleigh Harris had ever seen, and as the first advancing tide of evening shadow invited the butterflies to retreat, a sickening realization came over him. His host had not allowed cameras here. No one else would ever see the masterpiece he had seen—or believe it, for that matter.

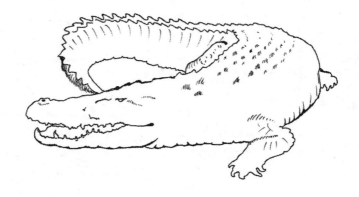

Pride of the Beast

The news on local stations that day began just as the summer rains had: slowly at first, but soon to reach a fever pitch. All along the Bayou that fateful August, thousands heard the once-gentle name "Katrina" and cringed. It was to be an unprecedented disaster, but few thought so yet.

*

Croc-a-Daddy Slim was the ruler of darkness and mayhem in a large section of the Big Easy, earning his name for his ability to repeatedly escape capture and prosecution, just like a writhing croc. Not only had Croc-a-Daddy been at odds with the police for years, but he was always looking over his shoulder in a constant game of cat and mouse with whoever was his latest rival. He had, in grisly ways, put down many who'd tried to invade his turf, including hiding the body of one hit in the netting of a balloon drop that, to the horror of many, tumbled down at midnight during a roaring New Year's Eve party.

Time was running out for him, though, as one by one he had trashed and alienated everyone around him, including his own mother. As the noose tightened and safe haven began to elude him time and again, he realized there was only one escape left. Croc-a-Daddy Slim must die.

He had seen it tried before and knew success was on his side. "Papa Moses" was the key—an undertaker, and the one man he could still trust. The one and only man who could make it all happen.

Through a careful plan—a stolen body, three hot cars, and an abandoned house—he would be able to pull off the ultimate deception.

That stormy August morning found him sitting in silent shadows in a basement, clutching two bags, staring at an old soap box, and thinking to himself, "What a funeral it will be!" People from all walks of life would line the streets of the French Quarter to see the pomp of a grand New Orleans sendoff. The procession would be filled with mourners whose eyes, he suspected, would be quite dry. Mostly, though, he imagined the sight of the casket itself—a special casket covered in crocodile skin, making its way slowly down the boulevard, causing a ripple of admiration as it went.

Instead, over the next several hours, the storm raged on, and Croc-a-Daddy Slim's funeral fantasy began to fade. Chagrined to find that the basement was beginning to fill, he reluctantly moved north into the main part of the house. To his amazement, after only a short while, water rose there also, forcing him to move to the second floor. Slow dread filled him as he grabbed his bags and finally shimmied out a window onto the roof of his now uncertain hideout. Hushed expletives escaped his mouth as he surveyed his surroundings through the storm, a torrent of chaos and mayhem. As far as he could see, houses were buried in water, and some had even broken loose from foundations and were floating dangerously free. The levy … was no more.

Suddenly he realized there was nothing left to do but hang on, as another house—or what was left of it—

headed right for him, bobbing wildly in the current. It arrived with a deafening fanfare, and Slim was flung free of all there was left to cling to.

He immediately abandoned his two bags filled with booty and began to tread the raging tide with great might. After managing to kick off his boots, he could swim in the madness for only a minute or two before realizing his strength was giving out. Swinging his head about to spy anything he might grab onto, he saw it—a small, empty boat quickly coming alongside him. He knew instinctively from the angle and speed that he could make it to the boat's side. At the precisely correct moment, he thrust out his hand and was able to grab hold of it and hoist himself up.

As he found the boat's safety, a flood of realizations came upon him all at once. This was no boat he saw beneath him now … it was a casket. His casket. It was unmistakable. He shook his head and sighed in wonder at the gnarled, rippled croc leather he rode upon. It was the last thing that Croc-a-Daddy Slim would ever see in this life, as a low-lying branch struck him squarely in the head and sent him to the depths of Katrina.

The Purple Tent

Mary tuned her radio just in time to hear the weatherman predict nothing but clear skies and warm temperatures that August morning.

"The fair will be just the ticket to chase away the doldrums," she thought as she rummaged through her closet looking for something cool to wear. She had gone to the local fair for years and always looked forward to all the sights, sounds, and smells it had to offer. She was well beyond the raucous rides, but she still relished a solitary perusal of a seemingly endless stream of exhibits.

She arrived in the early afternoon and parked, hearing the distant sounds of calliope and the low, rhythmic rumble of the carousel.

Four hours later, she found herself sitting on a grassy knoll, savoring every bite of a corn dog. Life for her had been a carnival of its own, full of transitions and surprises. Some had been good, some unnerving, but all she had met with a wise acceptance of what she had been dealt.

Mary looked across the crowd to a hodgepodge of booths and tents that seemed to fit no particular category. She spied among them a dark purple tent which, she could see, was want for wear, with tiny stars stitched to its side and a simple standalone sign keeping its entrance company. She glanced at it on and off the entire time she ate and was sure, after an hour, that not one person had gone inside. At last she rose and collected her things, deciding to give it a better look.

As she approached, her brow furrowed, and she cocked her head at what she thought perhaps was a joke. The entire sign was nothing but dozens of question marks in different sizes and colors. Amused, she stepped to the entrance, pulled aside the musty tapestry that guarded it, and entered a mostly dark room.

"There you are!" spoke an old voice from the other side of a table.

It was an old gypsy woman, wearing baubles and a silk scarf over her head. "If anyone in this world is a hundred years old, this woman is," thought Mary.

She sat down and spoke for a few minutes with the old mage, then she took out her purse and found a few bills, which she slid across the table. The old woman, in return, reached under the table and brought out a deck of cards. Mary thought they appeared to pre-date even the fortuneteller; they were old, worn, and at first glance, looked handmade.

The gypsy set the cards in front of Mary and asked her to cut and shuffle them as she pleased. Then she took them back and proceeded to lay them out, three rows of four cards each. Mary leaned forward and looked carefully at the beautiful symbols and figures depicted.

"I've never seen cards like these before," she said in wonder, looking down at them. "So! What does this mean for me?"

There was no answer, so she glanced up, only to find that the old woman had left the table and was standing in the shadows, pinching her lower lip and staring right at her. Mary raised her eyebrows and held up her palms as if to question this sudden departure. Slowly the old mage returned, sat down, and reached across the table to hold her hands. She looked deep into Mary's eyes, as if searching for something. After a long pause, finally spoke.

"When I was still quite young, my great-grandmother, then at the end of her life, summoned for me. She had been watching me closely from the time I entered this world, and she told me then that she saw in me 'the gift.' Many an hour I spent taking in all she had to bestow, until at last one day she declared my training complete. That day, she gave me three things: the curtain you see behind me, the mirror that hangs beside it, and these well-worn cards.

"Of course, she showed me many things about the cards and how they spoke, but the last thing she did with them was search for twelve cards in particular, which she then laid out on the table. She told me to memorize their exact order. I asked her their meaning, and she told me that there was no meaning—only this: that to whomever in my lifetime these cards, in this order, should be dealt, should be granted the wish of beholding their fondest desire.

"And so, young woman," the crone whispered, now looking down at the cards, "what is it you desire?"

There was a silence between the two, as Mary struggled to take it all in and search for some corner of her soul that would believe this impossible tale. Still, the greater part of her was coaxed to let go and play along. She sensed no danger in it. She knew, of course, what her wish would be. She had thought of it many times since childhood.

Mary told the old woman what it was, and the secret drew a delicious, wrinkled smile from her cheeks. "Step to the mirror, lass," she instructed, "and speak to it your desire. Then pull aside the curtain and step beyond to claim it."

Mary did as instructed. Stepping to the curtain, clutching it gently, and pulling it aside, she truly expected to see nothing but the fabric of the purple tent. What she actually saw took her breath away …

*

All around him, all his life, people had declared him a living wonder. He cared for no such stroking, craving only solitude, a good meal each day, and the means to bring to fruition the fountain of his desires. But his desires and visions were well beyond anyone else's in the wide world, and he struggled daily to bring to life all of his fantastic ideas. Most of his efforts brought forth no fruit, and again and again he was met with frustration.

Recently he had been pressed to capture the likeness of a young woman, whose beauty had at once struck him as peculiar.

After long preparation and thought, she was summoned to his studio, and after some formalities, he finally set his hand to begin. He sensed … greatness. He sensed something else, too—so strong and distinct that he immediately turned around and, addressing the shadowed corner of the room, he called out, "Who's there?"

There was no reply, nor was there ever to be one over the course of the project. From that first moment to the final finishing stroke years later, whenever he would set his hand to canvas, he would feel that someone was watching him. It was bothersome at first, but soon he accepted the feeling as a kind of invisible partner of the project, only to be missed when he at last finished and never felt it again thereafter.

*

Mary was baffled to find not the back of the tent, but a spacious, well-lit room. Amazed, she stepped softly forward, entering the room at a shadowed corner. She was able to see clearly all that was within it, which included an old, bearded man sitting comfortably behind an easel. Before him was a young woman who looked somehow familiar to Mary.

As the old man began to paint, he almost immediately set his brush back down and turned to the very corner where Mary was standing. "Who's there?" he demanded, brush raised, his brow wrinkled in confusion.

Mary somehow knew he could not see her, and though she did not understand his sharp words, she instinctively held her tongue. Soon after, the old man turned and began to paint once more. Then something happened that at first made Mary feel dizzy. His hands began to move faster and faster still, until everything around the canvas was just a blur. Light, lady, and painter moving about, even the room was changing from second to second. The only constant in her vision was the painting itself. No matter what, it stayed in the same place, in her line of sight, as it began to take shape, color, and form.

At last it was near finished, and the vision slowed until at normal speed, the master applied the final stroke. Mary had seen many stop-action films in her life, but nothing would ever compare to the three minutes she had just witnessed. Before her sat the unmistakable beauty and birth of none other than the Mona Lisa.

Moments later, in a dreamy haze, Mary brushed past the mystic on her way out of the purple tent. She was filled with awe and a new burning desire.

"Tell me, lass," the old woman queried, "what now?" The words hung like magic in the musty tent.

"Oh, me?" said Mary, pausing, a look of profound confidence spreading across her face. "Well, I am a painter ... and now I am going to paint *my* masterpiece."

A Week in Paradise

Kaleen Carson had always wanted to visit Africa. As a child, its natural beauty through movies, books, and the occasional documentary on television had fascinated her.

Television was her playground and her work now, as she had made her way from local commercials as a child, to newscaster as a young woman, finally to finding herself in most everyone's living room each week as the lead in a major legal drama. She had been married and divorced twice and had two grown children. Of late, she spent what very little time she had in decorating her West Coast home, and in the process she'd met a most amazing man.

The man, Luciano, had been born and raised a stone's throw from the Piazza in Venice, Italy. Having come to America as a young man, he had eventually found work as a beautician and then moved soon after, with a small investment, to the world of interior decorating. That business had been kind to him, to say the least; he had made a fortune many times over and amassed a who's who list of clients by the time he had turned forty.

But he had not found true love, or even the appearance thereof, until the day Kaleen walked into his shop one winter afternoon, and the room had begun to spin. Kaleen noticed his reaction right away, and she was used to it. But she was stunned to find, after a few minutes in conversation, that Luciano did not watch television, and so he had no idea who she was.

Over the weeks and months that passed after their meeting, Kaleen made several purchases, had a number of lunch dates with Luciano, and was thoroughly amused with the flamboyant Italian, who seemed to have endless talents. Luciano was more than amused—he was smitten, and after what he deemed a proper period of time, he offered her the only card he had left to win her heart: an invitation to his casbah in Morocco.

Sitting on fifteen acres of oasis twenty kilometers outside of Marrakech was Casbah Tamadot. Luciano had purchased the property and its one modest structure five years previous and turned it into a paradise he could escape to for four months out of the year. He had methodically added to the original structure, which had grown to nearly thirty thousand square feet, with twenty-two bedrooms, three dining rooms, and numerous sitting rooms, all adorned with his impeccable taste in décor. His two sisters had faithfully trained his staff in the fine art of Italian cuisine, and all who visited declared that this kind of hospitality was the kind money could not buy.

Kaleen cleared her schedule for a precious month and accepted the invitation: an eight-day stay in the world of Luciano. Only as she made travel arrangements did she realize, to her delight, that she would indeed be visiting Africa. Although she had traveled much of the world, she had never found the opportunity to breach the continent's massive borders. Now, as she was being ferried by a chauffeur through the outskirts of Marrakech, she felt that she had been transported back in time.

The casbah, and all it had to offer, was everything that she had expected and more—scrumptious meals, precious solitude, shopping at the souk, and marvelous company, all orchestrated by an ever-attentive host.

Luciano had entertained many at his fortress of hospitality and could tell that Kaleen was indeed charmed, yet he also knew that he had not yet won what he deemed most precious—her heart. He lay in his bed on the seventh night of her visit, pondering his desires and intentions. He could almost feel her indecision waft through his window, mixed with the cool, Moroccan air, feeling that if he had just *one more week* she would indeed be his. "Still time, though, for my secret weapon," thought Luciano as he drifted off, a faint smile on his face.

*

Pitka was normally the most obvious resident of the casbah, but she had been away the entire week Kaleen had been visiting, just returning the morning of her departure. She had been seeing a specialist in town for a pesky virus, but she was all better now and happy to be returning.

*

The morning of the eighth day, Kaleen looked out her bedroom window just in time to see a very large truck and trailer enter the courtyard. She wondered what all the hubbub was about, seeing most of Luciano's servants swarming around the trailer in great excitement. Her curiosity was finally sated when the doors were flung open, and out stepped its passenger: a nine-thousand-pound elephant. Kaleen gasped at the sight and felt a sudden thrill rise within her.

Luciano was down below, directing his servants, and he looked up to see Kaleen's sweet face peering out her window. "Come and meet my friend!" he called out, to the woman's delight.

Soon an elaborate saddle was carefully placed on Pitka's back, and after a few adjustments, she and her two human passengers were off for a short trip through Luciano's lush gardens. There, in small clearing, a table and umbrella had been set up for breakfast. They dismounted, leaving the elephant nearby as they sat down to enjoy the meal and each other's company.

"I've had such a wonderful time here. It's a shame I have to leave this afternoon," Kaleen said in between sips of mint tea.

"So stay another week," Luciano whispered, leaning forward.

Kaleen smiled and looked across the valley. Pitka swung her trunk, and Luciano motioned to a servant. "Pitka would like to join our breakfast, I believe," he said, grabbing a bucket of granola that had been brought over. "Would you mind feeding her?"

Kaleen reached into the container and grabbed a large handful. She walked over to the elephant and hesitantly raised her hand to its mouth.

"Don't be afraid," Luciano encouraged. "She's very gentle. Just put your hand right into her mouth."

Kaleen cautiously approached, and she squealed with delight as her hand indeed disappeared into the beast's mouth. It was both frightening and exciting—something powerful, yet gentle, such as she had never felt before.

Finally Pitka was through, and she released Kaleen's hand, turning to the bucket looking for more. Kaleen started to sit, and glancing at her hand, she made a shocking discovery. "It's gone!" she cried.

Luciano immediately rose and put his hand on her shoulder. "What, what?" he said.

"My ring, it's gone! Pitka ate it!"

"Oh my …"

"Yes, it's a family heirloom, and it's … oh nooooo!" Her voice trailed off in shock as she sat down in dismay, staring pale-faced at her now-bare finger, Luciano kneeling beside her.

"Listen now," he said with a quiet confidence, "I think everything will be fine."

"No, no, I need it back!"

"Yes, yes," Luciano comforted before adding, "Well you see, this happened once before, a few years back. A servant was feeding her and lost a bracelet. All was well, because the bracelet came out the other end just fine."

"Do you mean," Kaleen said, gaining hope, "that if I wait until tomorrow we will find it?"

"Oh yes, we will *definitely* find it," the man replied, "but it will be about a week."

The Sixth Stanza

As he climbed the last five hundred yards of his journey, William Cook heard a sound that would have made any record mogul cry for joy—had one been alive at the close of the nineteenth century. It was a quartet of monks that William mistook for angels, so sublime was their song as it drifted across the canyon.

He had spent three grueling days traversing streams and terrain that had taxed him to the point of exhaustion. He was a desperate man who knew somewhere inside that his only solace lay within the Monastery of the Five Stanzas.

Cook had journeyed through most of his life down in the proverbial gutter. He had taken on so many aliases over the years that his one true name was nearly lost to him. A criminal to all who swore allegiance to nothing but his selfish desires, as a young man something inside of him had begun to rot one day. The rot went unchecked until finally his very heart was lousy, with nothing but darkness and rage for the world.

Now in his early forties, he had recently become uneasy at the sight of blood on his handkerchief. He was told by a doctor he had only weeks to live. Most of his possessions he abandoned or sold, and there were no longer any friends or family to give a last farewell to.

*

The history of the Monastery of the Five Stanzas reached back some three hundred years, its teachings another thousand. It was rooted in the script of an ancient poem of love and devotion. Written originally in a long-lost language from a distant land, its alphabet was known now only to the handful of holy men who graced the barren plateau of sacred refuge among the rolling hills of California's coast.

The poem was five stanzas long and known not only by heart by each of the monks, but also by touch, for it was the very basis for a massage technique used by the monks to cure myriad ailments. There was a certain melodic chant that went also with the poem, and as one was treated, a monk would touch the body, actually tracing out with hands and fingers the original script while also singing each word softly as it was applied. Thus, treating a patient was referred to as "singing them a stanza." Each of the five stanzas treated a different part of the body, and in extreme occasions all five were "sung" in succession.

*

The abbot of the monastery sat at a simple wooden table and took in the pleasures of the midday sun peeking through his window. He had filled his sacred role for the past eighteen years now, and he always savored his moments of solitude. Although visitors here were few, and accommodations were sparse, the abbot found there was still much to attend to as the head of this band of brothers.

His duties included the arduous, personal training of each monk in their healing arts. He taught all he knew to his beloved fellows, holding back one secret only: a secret that had been taught to him from the deathbed of the previous abbot.

This particular day, news reached him of the new arrival, and after a brief brotherly conversation, it was deemed by him prudent to attend to the man himself. Mr. Cook's reputation preceded him even into the walls of this remote haven, and the abbot, ever protective of his charge, knew there was a possibility that he would have to ask the guest to leave.

A few minutes in conversation would allay his concerns. Here was a familiar man, he perceived—a man who had run the gauntlet of life and was worse for the wear. The fight in him was gone, and the only thing remaining was a bleakly voiced hope that the monk's fabled song could somehow cure him. The abbot gave no promises—no verbal reply at all—but invited him to a back room to bathe, drink tea, and lie on a modest cot of wool and straw.

Once his guest was prepared, the holy man entered and spoke to him in low tones. He rubbed his strong hands together and whispered a prayer before approaching the bed.

William had never been touched by either man or woman in such a fashion. For the first few minutes, he struggled even to relax, but soon he surrendered to the soft melody and the abbot's strong, firm touch.

Most of two hours later, William lay comfortably on his back and could see the abbot standing above him as the fifth stanza began. As the treatment approached its conclusion, the traveler began to feel a profound change come over him, a wash of emotion and realization running through him so powerful that he drew in a breath as if he had been underwater for years. Deep down, through the art of the healing song, a connection was restored—one that had been lost years ago: that of remorse.

Tears streamed down William's cheeks, tears of anguish and release, the abbot could not ignore. In that moment as he peered down at the outsider, wiping away the man's tears, the abbot came to a realization himself. Here at last he had found his long-lost brother, a soul that had become so caught up in the evils of the world that he had become unrecognizable—until now.

"Ah, Billy boy, you've come back," he whispered.

"My brother," said William as he reached up to embrace the other man and whispered his own message. "So many have I wronged, big brother, and so far have I strayed. I am loath to go on. Please, please, send me on my way."

The wise abbot, tears in his eyes, too, and with a love beyond this world, did just that. Rubbing his powerful hands together, he began singing a song that only he knew. It was a secret song he had been taught years ago, a song that would indeed send his brother's soul to another place. The song of the sixth stanza.

TC's Adventure

Winfred carefully descended the ladder that July afternoon to take a brief stroll and survey his progress. He, along with a few hundred more gardeners, tended to all that was necessary to keep Central Park—*the* Central Park—in tip-top shape.

His life had been shaped, pruned, and formed itself, the most notable influence being his father, now long gone, who had been a gardener himself. He had taught his son the art of shaping that which one planted and grew, mostly into beautiful geometric designs, but often into the form of whimsical topiaries. The most notable of these for Winfred was a large elephant, who had balanced a ball on its trunk for many years in their yard, to the great delight of the entire neighborhood.

Now in his fifties, Winfred lived in a small apartment with an old tomcat for his only companion. On most days, TC (short for "that cat") accompanied him to work among the greenness and seemed to take great delight in supervising his every move. After many years on the job, Winfred found himself the caretaker for a one-block-long section of the park, which bordered a busy avenue.

This early morning as he stood well back surveying his work, he could not help notice the pattern his trees made on the glass skyscraper just across the street. The combination of reflection and shadow, that morning, splayed the unmistakable shape of a horse's head. Amused, he climbed his ladder once again to trim a few more branches and, after several more trips back and forth, was tickled to see an entire horse emerge, big as day, on the building's side. Something from that moment on took his mind and soul into another place. He and TC would return each day for the next two weeks, until he had produced something truly amazing that really only the two of them could see.

True, anyone walking along the avenue could see, for a moment, the shape of a horse, but through his patience and quiet, Winfred was the only person who took in the full beauty of what he had done. After witnessing the magic for days, it suddenly struck Winfred just how he could share his masterpiece with the world.

That evening, Winfred visited a young friend for dinner, and after some instruction he went home with a video camera and a small tripod. He went early the next day to the roof of a municipal tool shed across from his row of trees, where he set up the camera, TC at his side with a curious look in his eyes. He set the camera, as he had been shown how to, to take just one frame every sixty seconds. He stayed for a short while to make sure it was working then began his short jaunt back to mete out his daily chores.

As he was leaving, Winfred noticed right away the absence of his cat. As the day wore on with no sign of TC, he felt only a mild, but ever increasing, sense of panic. By day's end he had sunk into a funk, having looked everywhere and asked anyone he could if they had seen his beloved companion, but to no avail. Finally, with heavy feet and a heavier heart at the close of the day, Winfred trudged to the shed to retrieve the borrowed camera.

That night, Winfred knocked on his young friend's door, tears streaming down his face and the borrowed camera clutched to his side. "TC is gone," was all he could muster as the door opened, and two firm hands reached out to embrace him, knowing full well what that cat meant to him.

After a cup of tea and more commiserating, Winfred's young friend attached the camera to his computer, and finally they were able to play in just a few minutes what the camera had been filming all day. Winfred was stunned.

*

That morning TC had watched as his human friend had placed the camera, and in his wise ways (for all cats are Zen masters), he had quietly stolen away and climbed the first tree in the row facing the great glass buildings, just as the sun was peeking through. The trees had been planted years ago and were spaced in such a way as to blend together, from one end of the block to the other. During the day, over and over again, TC would climb from one branch to another, then one tree to another, until he had traveled the entire length of the street, never having touched the ground. When day was done and darkness had finally come, he came down from the lofty branches and quietly strode off ...

*

As Winfred and his friend played the video, they saw just what they had been hoping for. In his patience, and drawing on all of his talents, Winfred had not just carved the foliage to splay the sun's rays in the shape of a horse on the side of a building. He had shaped all of the trees in turn so that as the day progressed, if you were patient enough to stand in one spot for eight hours and watch the side of the building, you could see the unmistakable *animation* of a horse in full gallop across the wall.

This, Winfred had expected to see. What made his heart leap for joy, though, was the unmistakable, small, flickering shape of a cat on the galloping horse's back, taking the ride of his life.

Kotaro

Yagyuro knelt on autumn leaves to wash at the edge of a stream he had never seen. All of his life he had prepared to fight and die, readying himself in the arts of the Bugei.

Peaceful times had stirred restlessness in many a samurai's soul, and in the absence of conflict, most found some solace in wandering the land in search of a duel—usually to the death.

Rising from the brook, Yagyuro gathered his sac and weapons and strode cautiously toward the next village. He was indeed a wanted man, yet he was content, lacking the sense of loneliness so often found in the masterless warriors of his day. Especially since he had such a helpful servant.

Kotaro had traveled with him for the last five years and was often busy at any task his master might need. On sweltering summer days, Kotaro would spend most of his time just keeping the flies at bay. At market, he busied himself with getting the attention of anyone his master would want to speak to and helped him to hide from those he wanted to avoid. If master's soup were too hot, Kotaro would cool it down; if his fire needed stoking, he would do that, too. And if his master needed nothing at all, sometimes Kotaro would dance about purely for his entertainment. It was no wonder that the wandering samurai was so content.

That night as the two of them lay sleeping in meager quarters, Yagyuro drifted off to a dream of a long-ago battlefield in a place far away. All around him soldiers swarmed and fought, yet an eerie silence filled the air, broken only by the distinct, simple sound of a tiny twig snapping.

Yagyuro immediately opened his eyes and came surprisingly awake. Noiselessly he rose from his bed, moving beside the door just as it began to open …

Into his room crept a figure dressed in black from head to toe, which moved as if floating toward his bed. As the intruder realized that the bed was empty, he spun quickly around, moonlight flashing across the Wakasashi blade he brandished and blinding Yagyuro for an instant. Instinctively now he moved toward the assassin even as deadly steel swung his way in the cool night air.

The blade whistled but did not find its mark, for Yagyuro, like a ghost, had suddenly appeared at the killer's side. The killer turned to strike again, but before his blade could even start its journey, ever faithful Kotaro leapt forward between the two and, with one stroke to the neck, felled the enemy at once.

As the failed assassin lay dying in the moonlight, he gazed up and saw the man who had bested him, standing alone and holding the most beautiful fan he had ever seen. It was a fan Yagyuro kept with him at all times, a fan that he had affectionately named … *Kotaro.*

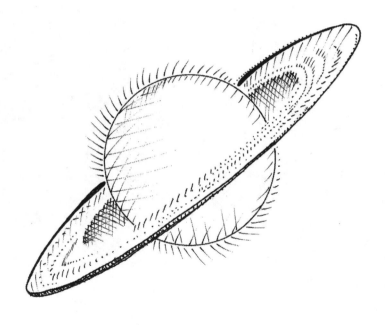

Piñata

The world had become sick with greed. For someone who had never set foot on earth, it was blazingly obvious.

Leedo sat alone in comfortable quarters and was never bored. Working as an astral-anthropologist far above our world had provided him with constant doses of tragedy, triumph, and humor. His home was far, far away, and it was comforting for him to be near a world so much like his, even though he knew he could never visit its surface. To do so was forbidden.

His spacious ship was cloaked from mankind's view by a powerful force emanating from its core. Nothing on earth came close to detecting it, the watcher knew. He sent back to his own world transmissions on a regular basis, and now, after many years of observing, he could not help but notice how very glum his reports had become. Like a spoiled child, the world was beginning to throw fits, he could see. Leedo gathered from his observations, though, that most humans were just tired of the greed. They were vowing to live in kinder, more giving times, but so far to no avail.

Through his monitoring of worldwide commerce, Leedo watched daily the tipping point of disaster come ever closer and could not help but feel twinges of mercy rise within him. He knew that a single transmission from his ship would put a halt to so much pain and suffering, but again and again his orders and code of conduct prevented him from action.

At length, after numerous ideas hatched and abandoned, Leedo one day found the answer that had eluded him for so many years, and he found it in a most unusual place: the rings of Saturn.

It was his secondary field of study, and a strange one, no doubt. He had visited Saturn's rings on numerous occasions and always been surprised and delighted with what he found there. Man had discovered many things about Saturn's rings from the time Galileo had first glimpsed them until now. Leedo, however, with far superior equipment, was able to see so much more. Spending countless hours, he had mapped their makeup and all that surrounded them.

On this particular trip his concentration was on what hovered on either side of the surprisingly thin ring: numerous "satellites." These were rock fragments ranging in size from basketball to boxcar. None of those he had mapped, however, were sufficient in size to be classified a proper moon.

Leedo moved with stealth and accuracy, eventually finding himself towing in his force field seven such satellites, and although many on earth gazed in his direction, his movement and gathering went wholly unnoticed. Easily breaking free of Saturn's orbit, his cargo in tow, he set out again for his primary place of interest, the earth. After only a short while, after making calculations that would have made even the brightest human scientists scratch their heads, he released his cargo, one by one. Then Leedo sat back to watch the show.

The rocks' spacing was uneven by design, but their aim was true. Only a few earth days later they were discovered by a young astronomer, who immediately sent his findings to a stargazer's clearinghouse for further study. Soon, the world's brightest minds convened to confirm what was initially feared: these chunks of matter, now dubbed "The Seven Dwarfs," would indeed collide with the earth in just a few short weeks.

Further study was conducted, though, and to everyone's relief, it was calculated that these fragments were small enough that they would most likely break up upon entering the atmosphere. In doing so they would create more of a light show, rather than what some at first had thought of as "the end of the world."

Of all who would watch on that fateful day in April as thousands of fragments would rain harmlessly down over the surface of the blue planet, none would be more entertained or curious to see the outcome than Leedo, the watcher of mankind. His careful eye and instruments had found seven objects that would indeed test the world's desire to abandon their greed and excess, for encased throughout those rocks to be spread out over the earth was no less than twenty-three metric tons of pure gold, waiting to be found.

Scentsational

The idea had begun in him during an innocent game of hide and go seek one day in a municipal park. His wife, Carol, had stopped to pick some roses for her hat, and Henry, who was mischievous by nature, had walked quickly on and hidden between two other bushes that were beginning to bloom.

As he waited to be found, a flood of wonderful emotions came upon him all at once. He recognized after a puzzled moment that the aroma of the two bushes he stood between had triggered this sudden reaction.

"It was beautiful—just beautiful, Carol," Henry mused as they walked on. "And yet standing there between those two bushes, I wondered why I felt so elated all of a sudden. Then it struck me."

"Oh? And what, pray tell, was that?" she asked, curious.

"It was all because of this!" Henry said, touching the tip of his nose. "Simply the *smell*, it was. That's what the beauty was all about."

The two walked on and talked of other such scents they had come across in life—scents that were both marvelous and disgusting, provocative and strange—and suddenly the idea was hatched: why not guide a tour based solely on smell? The prevailing industry in their coastal town was indeed tourist based; thousands flocked there every year, to its beauty, and for the numerous events held there annually. Henry and Carol even came up with a name for their unique endeavor: "The Scentsational Tour."

The weeks flew by as Henry and Carol traveled their majestic peninsula, collecting the smells and locations they'd use for the tour. Finally approaching the date of another major, tourist-attracting event, having made meticulous and strange arrangements all over town, they took out an ad, distributed flyers, and then sat back to wait. They were not disappointed, for just three days before the scheduled date, all twenty seats of the small bus they had hired were filled. The tour was on.

It was obvious to those that went that day that at many of the tour stops there was not much to see—but oh, what an olfactory feast it was!

The first stop, naturally, was nothing more than a walk between the two bushes Henry had originally found. It was a somewhat comical sight to see twenty grown men and women walking between them. They would wait to go between with confused looks on their faces, and they would emerge from the foliage with huge smiles.

Next they visited the back alley of a small chocolate factory, then was a walk through the kitchen of a famous restaurant, the surprises coming one after another. Then came a stop that actually brought tears to a few of the mens' eyes, a visit to the local high school boys' locker room. There, as the group stood, smelling a youthful sweat, Henry read aloud a moving speech that had been given by a coach years ago at a big game. The speech, delivered at halftime, had inspired his boys to go out and beat their rivals when the odds were clearly stacked against them.

The SPCA, a drive by the main pier where fishermen were bringing in their day's catch, a stroll down Main

Street during the local farmers' market, and several other stops brought again and again comments of a superlative nature from all who rode along.

The tour guides had saved the best for last, having spent the most time and effort seeking out and making arrangements for this final stop. They had timed their arrival to coincide with the setting of the sun over the bay, a small concession to the visual beauty that abounded there. It was a private beach that could be reached only by a small path that cut through the property of a young couple that Henry and Carol had met and gotten to know during their long preparations.

As the group walked out onto the small strand, they were invited to gather together on a large beach blanket that had been laid out for them, then stand and hold hands, close their eyes, and above all, *breathe deep.*

One of the older men, thoroughly caught up in the moment, shouted out, "Ah, to be young again!" He was echoed immediately thereafter by many of the others. Something powerful was here, no doubt they knew as they shook hands and embraced, sipped refreshments, and finally made their way along the trail back to the waiting bus.

*

Through the part of a curtain at a large window, a young man and woman watched the happy crowd gathered down below on their small, private beach. They smiled at one another, thinking of the great delights they had availed themselves of, just minutes before, on the very blanket where strangers now stood.

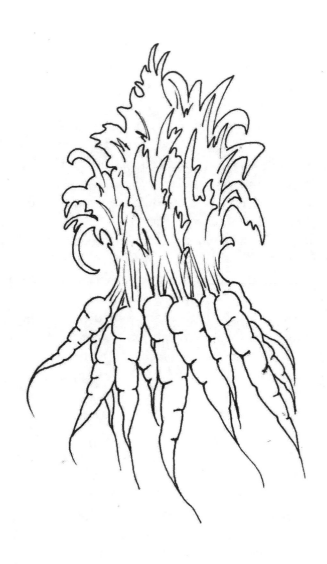

Carrot Soup

It was Tuesday, and for Celia that meant only one thing: the local farmers' market. Everything in its season was to be found there fresh, and in great abundance. Most of her meals, and even the beauty of her shop, revolved around what she found there, as she was most fond of fresh flowers, and she always found just the right ones to grace her shop each week.

This day, as she turned a people-packed corner, her eye caught a flash of orange that made her heart jump. Carrots. She saw lots of carrots each week, but something inside told her heart what her mouth moments later confirmed: these were indeed gold from the ground. As she savored the sampled carrot's goodness she remembered something her grandmother had taught her as a child: how to make carrot soup. For the next half hour she searched out everything else that would fill her kettle along with the carrots, and then she headed home to work her magic.

The next few hours flew by for Celia, and as always she found herself with much more soup than a single woman, like her, could eat—even in a week or more. After a brief search, she turned up a few jars, which she lovingly filled with her efforts, and then she set out once again on a mission of mercy.

She lived in a city that was so small in population that there were very few people she didn't know by sight—or for musicians, by sound. Eddy was one of the latter who lived less than a block away. As she drew near his door, Celia was surprised at the silence that came from within. Eddy was rarely without his mandolin; he carried it with him all around the house, indeed, everywhere he went.

Celia knocked twice before hearing a faint voice answer from within. Mildly alarmed, she gently opened the door and gingerly called out his name. She tip-toed through the cluttered apartment until she found Eddy, in bed moaning, his beloved instrument lying listlessly on the floor.

"Hey, you," he whispered. "Sorry I couldn't come to the door. It's just that I ..." he faltered. "I think I might pack it in, Celia."

"Oh, Eddy, my, my," she said as she took off her jacket and set down her bag. "See, I've brought you something!"

After a brief search for a saucer and a spoon, Celia began filling him, between sighs and ahhs, with her rich creation. With each spoonful, she could sense relief spread over him, as color returned to his cheeks.

"Who woulda thought!" exclaimed Eddy, sitting up in bed. "I tell ya, Celia, this soup is a lifesaver!"

After a few more bits of news, sure that he was on the mend, Celia was off again. She was much relieved to hear the happy plucking of a mandolin as she walked farther down the block, toward the sound of a roaring torch.

*

Peter had worked metal of all kinds since childhood and was used to seeing Celia at least once a day. They had met by chance at a soirée a few years back and had recently become fond of more than a polite kiss.

After setting his torch down and showing Celia what busied him this day, Peter noticed she had pulled from her bag a jar of soup, still quite warm. He had tasted many of her delights, but never had he seen or tried anything like carrot soup before. He was reticent as she opened the jar and dipped in her finger to give him a taste. Thoughts of baby food flashed through his mind as her carrot-coated finger was raised to his lips. For Peter, it was not a pleasant thought. He winced, but he held open his mouth nonetheless.

He was not prepared for what happened next. The soup, to him, was not only delicious, it also woke up something that had been sleeping inside of him—not a memory, but a desire that for a brief moment caught him off guard.

Celia noticed a bright flicker in his eyes and was about to say something, but before she could speak, Peter's hand was around her waist, and his lips were pressing with a gentle passion up against hers. After the kiss, he took a step back from Celia and looked at her as if searching for something. "Can I come by later on …? There's something I have to tell you," he whispered in her ear, leaning forward.

"Sure … how about seven?" Celia said as she strolled out of his shop, her bag a little lighter, her head a little in the clouds.

Peter turned toward a dusty shelf, pulled out a dog-eared phone book, and began paging through it looking for the J section. "J," he thought. "J for jewelers …"

The Waving Cat

My father has always been a fascination to me. A world traveler and natural entertainer, as a young man he balanced tables and chairs on his chin and sang exotic French songs in variety shows to work himself through college.

Whatever was new or exciting—and certainly unusual—he was sure to discover it, and my siblings and I were sure to hear about and often experience it, too. Whether it was biorhythm, handwriting analysis, divining rods, or old Hitchcock movies, we were ever his captive audience, waiting for the next "wow" that lay right around the corner.

Eight years ago, after numerous tests and doctor visits, he was shipped off to a special facility up north, where he went through the greatest trial of his life: quintuple bypass surgery. Today he leads a happy, quiet life not far from where I live. I see him often now and take him each week for drives to familiar places. Places that he recognizes less and less. He suffers from Alzheimer's, with a little dementia tossed in there, too.

My father has thrown my family more than one curveball lately, but one in particular is his incessant gift giving. Until he could drive no longer, he would take trips to the Goodwill store, clearing out their "kitsch" department, sometimes twice a week. Soon the storage space beneath my parents' stairs was bulging with stacks of plastic bags full of the stuff. Over the next few years, I became the beneficiary of most of it, graciously accepting his loving gestures and placing the items in larger bags, which eventually found their way into a dusty loft in my shop. The gifts are coming less frequently now, and today each time I walk into my shop, I look fondly up at the numerous bags, which to me are a testament to his incredible, generous spirit.

"I have an item for you!" my father announced from his stairwell a few weeks ago during one of my visits. "You will love it, love it, love it!" he assured me as he made a huge gesture with a downturned finger, indicating that I should follow him downstairs.

I did, as he limped down the stairs with his one bad knee, a now familiar routine that I have come to accept with as much grace as possible.

"Here," he said, thrusting something shiny toward me. "I don't need it anymore."

This was what he usually said, and I never argued with him. Indeed it seemed to me that in his condition he had little use for most of the belongings he had acquired in life. This particular trinket was one of those Japanese waving cats that are produced by the millions, its one paw raised up in the air, pivoting back and forth endlessly, its motion fueled by two small batteries hidden under its feet. I knew from friends of mine the meaning of the constant paw-wave: the rocking limb was "catching money" and symbolized prosperity.

I took the cat from my father and admired it as if I had never seen one before. I tipped the paw with my finger to set it in motion, and it waved, but it stopped much too soon. "No batteries," I thought as I looked underneath.

But there were indeed two batteries, I observed, rusting away side by side. It was obvious then to me: this cat had run out of prosperity for the moment, perhaps forever. Later, as I got into my car to leave, I put him in the little change tray beneath the dashboard and gave his paw another flick. Nothing.

For the next week, there it sat, in an ever-growing pile of loose change and nic-knacks. Every time I got into my car, I could not resist giving the cat's paw a push.

"One of these days, I'll have to get some new batteries," I kept thinking.

*

Yesterday morning, I trudged into my shop to look around and see what I might finish—and hopefully get paid for. Making a living as a metal sculptor is a precarious endeavor most days. After a bleak assessment, I walked back to my car to make another trip to the hardware store. I plopped down into the driver's seat, only to make a startling discovery ... the cat was *waving*. At first I thought that my motion and weight had temporarily moved it and that as always, the cat's paw would stop in just a few seconds. It did not, and I sat there stunned at the steady click, click, click, as it waved away, my car now completely at rest.

Just then, my cell phone rang. I fished it out of my pocket and opened it, still staring at the cat.

"Hello, sir?"

"Yes?"

"This is Julie, from the Kearns accounting firm ... we have a check here for you in the amount of fifteen hundred dollars. Would you like to come pick it up today?"

Afterword

It has always been my pleasure to talk to people about my stories after they have read them and discuss where the ideas came from. Some of them came out of left field, and whatever sparked the idea is gone, only the story itself remaining. Others are quite vivid ...

"Purr-haps" was written immediately after waking from a dream in which this story was played out as nearly as I could remember. My wife, Catherine, had had a cat named Ozzie, who had passed on before we met. Perhaps this was my way of meeting him (no pun intended).

The idea for "The Inheritance" had been in my mind for several weeks when I found myself invited to an impromptu dinner party, only to find out that each of us were obliged to read something at the end of the meal. I excused myself to the living room and in about fifteen minutes wrote, on Post-it notes, the story you see in this book.

The possibility of an athlete coming out of nowhere to win a major event has always fascinated me. "The Golden Prize" was the result.

Once, on a visit to a spa, I spied a banana tree that had just such a flower as described in "Friends." I imagined what would happen if the tree noticed me as much as I could not help but notice it.

"The Sleep Talkers" was a coupling of two different stories. The first idea was of a couple who met late in life and who were somehow able to go back in time and see each other as teenagers. I had thought about this premise for quite some time, but it didn't seem to be going anywhere. A second idea I had was about two people who talked to each other in their sleep. I asked myself, "What would they say, and who would hear them, and why?" Putting these two ideas together made it all work at last.

The idea for "The Purple Tent" was born in my sculpture studio. I was melting bronze with my torch to produce a particular sculpture when it struck me: this is a show unto itself, and I am the only one who is enjoying it. We have the art of the masters before us to enjoy, but who had the privilege to actually watch them work?

"A Week in Paradise" is taken from my own travels to Morocco to visit a man with whom I worked for many years. His palace, far up the valley from Marrakech, was more spectacular than I could ever describe, and it is owned and run today as a fabulous resort by Sir Richard Branson. Recently my friend, (named Luciano in real life just like the story) invited me over for dinner and to say good-bye. I am grateful I had the opportunity to read the story to him and get his approval before he passed on. I will miss him dearly, but death and time can never diminish the hospitality and kindness he showed me. Truly, as was stated in the story, "His kind of hospitality was the kind money could not buy."

"Piñata," though admittedly possibly the most far-fetched story in the collection, was the one of which my mother commented, "Yeah, that could happen!" In fact, this past year marked the very first time in history that we humans have spotted an object in space (which was about the size of a car) two weeks before it entered our atmosphere and broke up harmlessly, scattering across the African desert.

I was the man in "Scentsational" who, "mischievous by nature, had walked quickly on and hidden between two other bushes that were beginning to bloom." I came up with the idea pretty much the way it is described in the story, by exploring in conversation with Catherine how powerful our sense of smell is.

The creative process, and how we choose to define it in today's world, intrigues me more and more each day. That "ah-ha" moment is my favorite part of the process, but funnily, some of the stories with the best "ah-ha" moments were ones that I, at one time, had dismissed as too fantastic or sentimental. "TC's Adventure" is one example. The idea that Winfred would create such a fantastic piece of art, I could see in my mind. It was just figuring out how one would describe such a thing that I could not fathom at first. In this case and many others, I can see now that it took courage and the permission from one part of me to another—to cross out sentences, or even whole sections, that I didn't like at first.

My little black and white notebook is still full of ideas for stories yet to be written, some of which I glance at from time to time and dismiss, for now—until they have fully ripened in my mind. Among the many yet to be finished is an idea for a two-part sequel to "The Sixth Stanza" with the tentative title, "Have You Ever Wrestled a Bear?"

Many of the others printed here have their own unique origins also, but if you absolutely must know them, or if you want to get some teasers of stories to come, then you'll have to come to Sand City and hunt me down. But be warned, I have to tell you … I can be mighty hard to find most days. In fact, people around here ask me all the time if I ever work, because they don't see me as often as they'd like. Fact is, I live right across the street from my sculpture studio and have a big hammock on a deck there. You never know when the mood will strike you to daydream for a bit.